Little Red Riding Hood

Picture Window Books
Minneapolis, Minnesota

First published in the United States in 2010
by Picture Window Books
151 Good Counsel Drive
P.O. Box 669
Mankato, Minnesota 56002
www.picturewindowbooks.com

©2005, Edizioni El S.r.l., Treiste Italy in CAPPUCETTO ROSSO

Printed in the United States of America.

All books published by Picture Window Books
are manufactured with paper containing
at least 10 percent post-consumer waste.

Library of Congress Cataloging-in-Publication Data
Piumini, Roberto.
[Cappuccetto Rosso. English]
Little Red Riding Hood / by Roberto Piumini; illustrated by Alessandro Sanna.
p. cm. — (Storybook classics)
ISBN 978-1-4048-5647-9 (library binding)
[1. Fairy tales. 2. Folklore—Germany.] I. Sanna, Alessandro, 1975– ill. II. Little Red
Riding Hood. English. III. Title.
PZ8.P717Li 2010
398.20943'02—dc22

[E]   2009010429

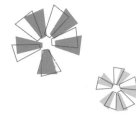

Little Red Riding Hood

Retold by
Roberto Piumini

Illustrated by
Alessandro Sanna

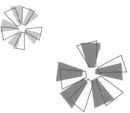

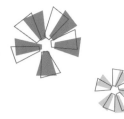

Once upon a time, there was a little girl who lived in a small village with her mother. The little girl often visited her grandmother, who lived deep in the woods.

The grandmother loved the little girl very much and gave her a red velvet riding hood as a gift. The little girl loved her riding hood, and she wore it day and night. So everyone called her Little Red Riding Hood.

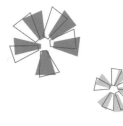

One day, Little Red's mother said to her, "Take this basket of treats to your grandmother. Go right away, walk quickly, and never leave the path."

"Yes, Mother," said the little girl. She picked up the basket and hurried off to her grandmother's house in the woods.

When Little Red was deep in the forest, a wolf saw her and greeted her.

"What's your name, little girl?" asked the wolf. "And where are you going all by yourself?"

"I'm Little Red Riding Hood," she said. "I'm taking some treats to my grandmother."

"Where does your grandmother live?" asked the wolf.

"Under the big oak tree in the forest," said the girl.

Ah, what a delicious snack she would make! the wolf thought to himself, his mouth watering. *If I am clever and careful, I can eat the grandmother first and have Little Red for dessert!*

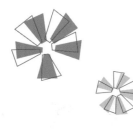

Little Red and the wolf walked together for a while. Then the wolf said, "Look at those lovely flowers! I'm sure your grandmother would love to have some."

Little Red stopped. She loved flowers, and so did her grandmother. The girl picked a few from the side of the path, then a few more a little farther away. With each flower she picked, there seemed to be a more beautiful one just a step away.

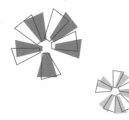

Meanwhile, the wolf ran to the grandmother's house and knocked on the door.

"Who is it?" asked the old woman.

"It's Little Red Riding Hood, Grandmother! I've brought you some treats," the wolf said.

"Open the door and come inside, my dear!" said grandmother.

The wolf opened the door, ran inside, and gobbled up the grandmother whole.

Then he put on her stocking cap, climbed into her bed, and pulled the bedsheets right up to his hairy chin.

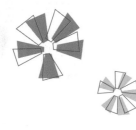

When Little Red Riding Hood's hands were filled with flowers, she went back to the path to hurry toward her grandmother's house.

When she arrived at the house, the door was open so she walked inside. In the dim light, she saw her grandmother in bed with her stocking cap on, looking very different than normal.

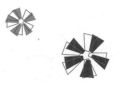

Little Red Riding Hood stepped closer to the bed. "Grandmother, what big ears you have!" she said.

"All the better to hear you with, my dear," said the wolf.

"Grandmother, what big eyes you have!" Little Red said.

"All the better to see you with, my dear," said the wolf.

"And grandmother . . . what big teeth you have!" said Little Red, frowning.

"All the better to eat you with!" howled the wolf.

Then he jumped out of the bed and swallowed Little Red Riding Hood in a single gulp.

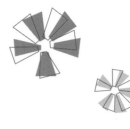

Feeling full, the wolf lay down on the bed again and fell asleep.

A little later, a hunter passed by, and he heard the loud snores. He thought to himself, *The old lady is snoring very loudly! Maybe she's sick. I'd better take a look.*

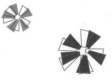

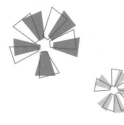

The hunter walked in and saw the wolf lying in bed. He realized that the wolf must have eaten whoever lived in the house. So he cut open the sleeping wolf with his knife. Out hopped Little Red Riding Hood and her grandmother!

"That evil wolf swallowed us up," said Little Red. "Thank you so much for saving our lives!"

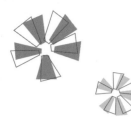

The hunter looked down at the wolf. "We can't let this wolf eat anyone else," he told Little Red. "Go and get some large stones and bring them to me."

So Little Red went outside and walked to a nearby lake. She gathered twelve large stones and brought them, one by one, to the hunter.

The hunter stuffed the stones into the sleeping wolf's belly. Then he stitched up the wolf with a needle and thread.

"That will teach him to eat grandmothers and little girls," the hunter said.

Then the three of them hid and waited.

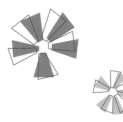

When the wolf woke up, he felt much heavier than before. He dragged himself outside and inched his way down to the lake for a drink. But the stones in his stomach made him so heavy that he fell into the water and sank to the bottom of the lake.

Back at the cottage, Little Red Riding Hood, her grandmother, and the hunter celebrated.

And the wolf was never seen again.

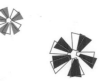

FAIRY TALE
Follow-Up

1. Little Red's mother told her to stay on the path on the way to her grandmother's house, but the girl did not listen. Do you think she would have been safer if she had followed her mother's rule?

2. Was Little Red scared of the wolf? Would you have been scared?

3. Who is the hero of this story? What did he or she do that makes them the hero?

4. Have you ever read another version of Little Red Riding Hood? Was the ending different? Were there other differences?

Glossary

celebrated (SEL-uh-brayt-ed)—did something special, such as had a party

cottage (KOT-ij)—a small house, often in a country setting

delicious (di-LISH-uhss)—very pleasing to taste

gobbled (GOB-uhld)—ate very quickly and greedily

howled (HOULD)—cried out like a wolf or dog

WRITE YOUR OWN
Fairy Tale

Fairy tales have been told for hundreds of years. Most fairy tales share certain elements, or pieces.
Once you learn about these elements, you can try writing your own fairy tales.

Element 1: The Characters

Characters are the people, animals, or other creatures in the story. They can be good or evil, silly or
serious. Can you name the characters in *Little Red Riding Hood*? There is the wolf, the hunter, the
grandmother, and the main character — Little Red Riding Hood.

Element 2: The Setting

The setting tells us *when* and *where* a story takes place. The *when* of the story could be a hundred years
ago or a hundred years in the future. There may be more than one *where* in a story. You could go from
a house to a school to a park. In *Little Red Riding Hood*, the story says it happened "once upon a time."
Usually this means that it takes place many years ago. And *where* does it take place? In the forest and
at Grandmother's house.

Element 3: The Plot

Think about what happens in the story. You are thinking about the plot, or the action of the story.
In fairy tales, the action begins nearly right away. In *Little Red Riding Hood*, the plot begins when the
mother tells Little Red to take some treats to her grandmother. She says, "Go right away, walk quickly,
and never leave the path." And the story takes off from there!

Element 4: Magic

Did you know that all fairy tales have an element of magic? The magic is what makes a fairy tale different from other stories. Often, the magic comes in the form of a character that doesn't exist in real life, such as a giant, a scary witch, or in the case of *Little Red Riding Hood*, a talking animal.

Element 5: A Happy Ending

Years ago, fairy tales ended on a sad note, but today, most fairy tales have a happy ending. Readers like knowing that the hero of the story has beaten the villain. Did *Little Red Riding Hood* have a happy ending? Of course! The hunter tricked the wolf, who sank to the bottom of the lake with a belly full of rocks. Then Little Red celebrated with her grandmother and the hunter.

Now that you know the basic elements of a fairy tale, try writing your own! Create characters, both good and bad. Decide when and where their story will take place to give them a setting. Now put them into action during the plot of the story. Don't forget that you need some magic! And finally, give the hero of your story a happy ending.

ABOUT THE Author

Roberto Piumini lives and works in Italy. He has worked with children as both a teacher and a theater actor/entertainer. He credits these experiences for inspiring the youthful language of his many books. With his crisp and imaginative way of dealing with every kind of subject, he keeps charming his young readers. His award-winning books, for both children and adults, have been translated into many languages.

ABOUT THE Illustrator

Alessandro Sanna is a writer and illustrator of children's books. Many of his picture books retell famous stories and plays. He likes experimenting with different techniques, but he loves traditional painting. Often, Sanna's choice of color and style are inspired by famous painters. When he's not working on his own projects, Sanna teaches creative drawing to both children and adults.

More Tales to Treasure

Open a Storybook Classic and experience the world of traditional fairy tales told through simple prose and splendid artwork. These safe and inventive picture books feature beautiful and whimsical illustrations that will charm young and old alike.

STORYBOOK Classics
Cinderella
Retold by Roberto Piumini
Illustrated by Raffaella Ligi

STORYBOOK Classics
Snow White
Retold by Roberto Piumini
Illustrated by Anna Laura Cantone

STORYBOOK Classics
Hansel and Gretel
Retold by Roberto Piumini
Illustrated by Anna Laura Cantone

STORYBOOK Classics
GOLDILOCKS and the Three Bears
Retold by Roberto Piumini
Illustrated by Roberta Sabayon

STORYBOOK Classics
Pinocchio
Retold by Roberto Piumini
Illustrated by Lucia Salemi

STORYBOOK Classics
Puss in Boots
Retold by Roberto Piumini
Illustrated by Francesca Chessa

STORYBOOK Classics
THE 3 LITTLE PIGS
Retold by Roberto Piumini
Illustrated by Nicoletta Costa

WAIT!
DON'T CLOSE THE BOOK!
THERE'S MORE!

FIND MORE:

Games & Puzzles
Heroes & Villains
Authors & Illustrators

www.CAPSTONEKIDS.com

STILL WANT MORE?

Find cool websites and more books like this one at www.FACTHOUND.com.
Just type in the BOOK ID: 9781404856479 and you're ready to go!